A Fairytale Treasury

This is a Parragon book
This edition published in 2000

Parragon
Queen Street House
4 Queen Street
Bath BA1 1HE UK

Produced by
The Templar Company plc
Pippbrook Mill
London Road
Dorking, Surrey RH4 1JE UK

Printed and bound in Italy
ISBN 0 75253 474 2

A Fairytale Treasury

Contents

Mary, Mary, Quite Contrary

Tom Thumb

The Steadfast Tin Soldier

Sing a Song of Sixpence

Hansel and Grettel

Rumpelstiltskin

Diddle, Diddle, Dumpling

The Sorcerer's Apprentice

Jack and the Beanstalk

Little Jack Horner

Hey! Diddle, Diddle

Hey! diddle, diddle,
The cat and the fiddle,
The cow jumped over the moon;
The little dog laughed
To see such fun,
And the dish ran away with the spoon!

CINDERELLA

Once upon a time there was a girl called Cinderella. She lived with her kind father, her wicked stepmother, and her two mean and ugly stepsisters.

Her stepmother made Cinderella do all the housework, and wait on her and her lazy daughters hand and foot.

Cinderella had to sleep on a straw bed in the attic, while her stepsisters had beautiful rooms, with soft beds and satin sheets. Cinderella worked hard every day and did not complain to her father in case she upset him.

Her stepsisters called her Cinderella, because at night she would sit dreaming by the warm cinders of the kitchen fire. But even though she dressed in rags she was a hundred times prettier than her bad-tempered sisters in their lovely gowns.

One day an invitation from the Prince arrived from the Palace. He was holding a Grand Ball. The ugly sisters were delighted and spent days trying on dresses and planning what to wear to catch the Prince's eye.
On the day of the Ball, Cinderella ran backwards and forwards between them, helping them to get ready. All the time they teased her because she was not allowed to go too.
"Ho, ho!" they chuckled. "How everyone would admire your lovely tattered dress! What a shame you cannot come with us!" And so they continued until at last they were ready, and they flounced away to the Ball. Cinderella sadly watched them go, then put her head in her hands and cried. "I wish that I could go to the Ball too," she sobbed. Little did she know that her fairy godmother was listening.

"I have come to grant your wish," said the fairy, appearing before her. "Fetch a large pumpkin from the garden." Surprised, Cinderella did as she was told and when her godmother tapped the pumpkin with her magic wand it turned into a golden coach!

Next she turned six grey mice into six fine white horses, a fat rat into a jolly coachman, and six lizards into footmen. Cinderella could hardly believe her eyes! With a last wave of her wand, the fairy godmother turned Cinderella's tatters into a lovely silver dress, with sparkling glass slippers on her feet. Cinderella was delighted! But as she climbed into the coach, her godmother warned that she must leave before midnight or everything would change back to what it had been before. With a smile and a wave, Cinderella promised not to forget.

When she arrived the Prince ran to welcome her, for she was certainly the most beautiful girl at the Ball, and as he led her into the ballroom everyone stopped to stare at her in admiration. As she passed her ugly sisters she held her breath, but they were so amazed by her beauty that they did not recognise her. The Prince could not take his eyes off Cinderella. He held her tightly in his arms and they danced all evening.

She felt so happy that she forgot all about the time. Suddenly the clock started to strike midnight! Cinderella fled from the room and out of the Palace. As she ran down the steps towards her coach one pretty glass slipper fell from her foot. Just as she reached it, the fine coach disappeared, and in its place stood the pumpkin. Pulling her tattered old cloak around her, Cinderella slipped away into the night.

Later her stepsisters came home and told her all about the mysterious beauty the Prince had danced with all evening. The only clue to her identity was a glass slipper she had left behind.

Next day the Prince issued a Royal Proclamation. He would search the land until he found the girl whose foot fitted the slipper and then he would make her his bride. The Court footmen visited every house in the country, but no one had a foot dainty enough to fit the slipper. Finally they arrived at Cinderella's home. The ugly sisters puffed and panted as they tried in vain to make the little slipper fit. Then it was Cinderella's turn. The ugly sisters gasped as it slipped onto her foot. It was a perfect fit!

Just then Cinderella's fairy godmother appeared and in a flash she was once again dressed in her finery. Much to her sister's dismay, the Prince married Cinderella the very next day and, as with all good fairy tales, they lived happily ever after.

★ Aladdin and the Magic Lamp ★

Once upon a time a poor tailor died, leaving his wife and an only son, Aladdin. One day, a stranger came to town claiming to be Aladdin's long-lost uncle, but he was really a wicked magician. Over supper, Aladdin's mother begged him to find work for her son and he gladly agreed, saying, "Tomorrow he can work for me!"
The next day the magician took Aladdin for a long walk outside the city.

"We are here," he said at last, and they stopped for a rest. Then he muttered a magic spell and the earth split open, revealing a stone with a brass ring in it. The magician pulled the stone back to reveal a flight of steps leading down out of sight.
"At the bottom you will find a lamp," said the magician. "Bring it to me and I will reward you well." Then he gave the boy a magic ring to protect him.

Aladdin soon found the lamp and returned to his uncle. "Hurry up and give the lamp to me!" said the magician impatiently, but there was something in his voice that made Aladdin hesitate and he refused to come out. The magician was furious, for a special magic prevented him from entering the cave himself. Yet he wanted the lamp more than anything, for he knew its magic could make him rich and powerful. Cursing, he slammed the stone slab shut and fled, leaving Aladdin trapped in the cave. Poor Aladdin sat weeping and, as he did so, he accidentally rubbed the magic ring. With a puff of smoke, a huge Genie appeared. "What is your wish?" thundered the Genie. "I am the Slave of the Ring and will obey you." Aladdin begged to be taken home and soon found himself back with his mother.

"Why would the wicked man want this old lamp?" she wondered and she gave it a rub.

With a huge flash, another great genie appeared, saying: "I am the Genie of the Lamp! I will grant your every wish!" Aladdin was delighted, as he had fallen in love with the Sultan's daughter. Perhaps the Genie could help him win her hand in marriage? He asked the Genie for a bag of fine jewels and his mother visited the Sultan with them. The Sultan was amazed, but his chief adviser, the Grand Vizir, was not pleased. He wanted the Princess to marry his own son, so he persuaded the Sultan to set a difficult task for Aladdin, to prove himself worthy. The Sultan asked for forty golden bowls filled with jewels, carried by forty fine slaves. Aladdin summoned the Genie and soon slaves with bowls of gems were marching through the palace gates. The Sultan gave Aladdin his blessing at once.

Aladdin called on the Genie of the Lamp. "I need a
set of clothes fit for a Prince, and a palace for
us to live in." The new palace was magnificent.
The walls were gold and
silver, set with diamonds.
Soon Aladdin and the
Princess were
married, and they
were very happy.
But far away,
the magician had
not forgotten
the magic lamp
and after many
years he returned
to the city to find
it. He soon learnt
of Aladdin's
wealth and
happiness, and
knew it must be
the work of the
lamp, so he made
a plan to win
it back.

The magician waited until Aladdin was away from home. Then he disguised himself as a merchant and knocked on the Palace door, offering to sell new lamps for old. The Princess was only too happy to get rid of Aladdin's old lamp, little realising its true worth. The magician snatched it and hurried away, busily plotting his revenge.

The next day the Sultan was horrified to find that the palace and his daughter had disappeared. The magician had ordered the Genie to take them to his home in Africa.
The Grand Vizier declared Aladdin must be an evil sorcerer. The angry Sultan gave Aladdin forty days to find her or he would be put to death. Aladdin was heartbroken and wept bitterly. As he did so, he rubbed his magic ring. In a flash the Genie appeared.

"Take me to the Princess," begged Aladdin
and at once he was in her room and she
told him all that had happened. Then
Aladdin understood.
The Genie of the Lamp had a
new master. Carefully he handed the
Princess a small packet
of powder.
"Pour this poison into the
magician's wine," he said,
"and all our troubles will
be over."

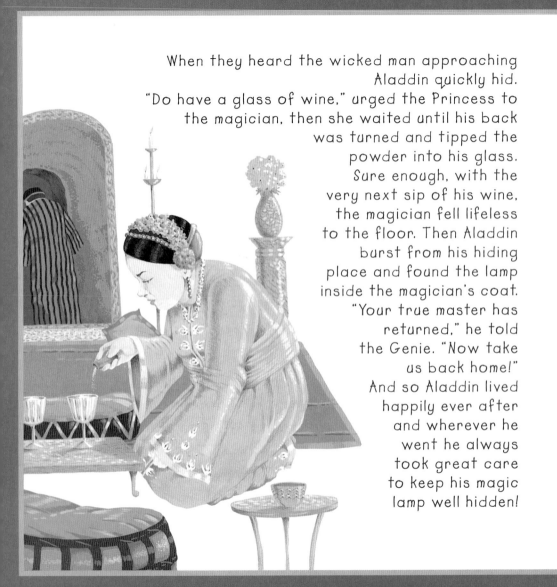

When they heard the wicked man approaching Aladdin quickly hid.
"Do have a glass of wine," urged the Princess to the magician, then she waited until his back was turned and tipped the powder into his glass. Sure enough, with the very next sip of his wine, the magician fell lifeless to the floor. Then Aladdin burst from his hiding place and found the lamp inside the magician's coat. "Your true master has returned," he told the Genie. "Now take us back home!" And so Aladdin lived happily ever after and wherever he went he always took great care to keep his magic lamp well hidden!

Rock-a-Bye, Baby

Rock-a-bye, baby, on the tree top;
When the wind blows, the cradle will rock;
When the bough breaks, the cradle will fall;
Down will come baby, cradle and all.

RAPUNZEL

There once lived a man and his wife who were good, kind people, but they were unhappy, as they longed for a child. The woman grew so sad that she fell ill and took to her bed. From her window she could see fresh green herbs growing in the garden of the big house that stood next door, and begged her husband to fetch some to make her better. The house belonged to a witch and the garden was surrounded by a high wall to keep everyone away. That night the man climbed the wall to take some of the herbs for his wife to eat, but the furious witch was waiting!

She agreed to let him go on one condition - that if they should have a child they would give it to her. The man was so terrified that he agreed and ran for home.

Some months later, his wife had a baby daughter and they were overjoyed. But soon after her birth the witch came and took the little baby away. The man and his wife were grief-stricken but how ever hard they searched, they could not find her. The witch raised the little girl all alone and named her Rapunzel. When Rapunzel was sixteen the witch locked her away in a tall tower in the middle of the forest and each day she would visit her and call out: "Rapunzel, Rapunzel, let down your hair!" Then Rapunzel would let down her two long plaits of golden hair from the window and the witch would climb up.

Then one day a Prince came riding through the forest and heard Rapunzel singing sweetly. He hid behind a tree when the witch arrived and watched as she clambered up into the tower. He thought Rapunzel was the most beautiful girl he had ever seen, and so when the witch had gone, he went to the tower and called: "Rapunzel, Rapunzel, let down your hair!" Then he climbed up Rapunzel's plaits and jumped inside the room. Rapunzel was astonished to see this handsome stranger, but she fell in love at once and agreed to be his bride. Soon they they had planned her escape. Each day the Prince brought her silk thread which she weaved into a ladder, and carefully hid away.

But one day she let slip about the Prince, and the witch was furious! She took out a pair of scissors and cut off Rapunzel's beautiful golden hair. Then she took Rapunzel away into a wilderness and left her there all alone.

That evening the witch lay in wait for the Prince, who called out: "Rapunzel, Rapunzel, let down your hair!" The witch tied Rapunzel's plaits to a hook on the wall and threw them out of the window. In a flash the Prince had scrambled up and leapt inside, but what a shock he got to find the horrible witch awaiting him, instead of Rapunzel! "Ha, ha, ha!" she cackled. "I have hidden Rapunzel far away and you will never see her pretty face again."

The Prince was filled with despair and leapt from the window. He landed in a rose bush and was blinded by the sharp thorns. Away he wandered into the forest, weeping for his lost love. He strayed through the wilderness for many weeks and with each step his heart grew heavier and heavier.

Then one day he heard someone singing sweetly. He had heard that song once before. Could it be Rapunzel? He stumbled blindly towards the sound and Rapunzel looked up and saw her Prince at once. She ran into his arms and held him close. As she wept for joy two of her tears dropped on his eyes and suddenly he could see once more!

"You will never be parted from me again," he promised Rapunzel, and so they made their way to his kingdom and there they were married. They heard no more from the wicked witch and Rapunzel and her Prince lived happily ever after.

The Little Mermaid

Once there was a little mermaid Princess, who lived with her father, The Mer King, and her five older sisters, in a beautiful coral palace beneath the sea. She loved her life under the sea, but she often daydreamed about visiting the world above the waves. Then, at sunset on her fifteenth birthday, she was allowed to visit the surface at last.

She watched spellbound as a fine ship came sailing by. Out on deck she could see a handsome Prince looking out to sea.
Suddenly there was a loud clap of thunder and dark storm clouds gathered. The waves rose high and the ship was tossed up and down, before finally sinking into the sea.

The little mermaid was very frightened, but she knew she must save the Prince. She found him clinging to a plank of wood, and gently carried him to shore.
As he lay upon the beach a young girl found him and called for help. The Prince opened his eyes and believed that she was the one who had saved him.

Only the little mermaid,
hiding behind a rock,
knew the real truth. Before
the Prince could ask who
she was, the young girl
ran off.

But the little mermaid could
not forget him and every
evening she swam to the surface of
the sea and gazed at the palace
where he lived.
"Come home with us," said
her sisters, but the
mermaid longed to
catch another
glimpse of the
Prince.

"You cannot share his life," her sisters told her. "You have a silver tail and will never be able to walk on dry land. You must forget him." But the mermaid could think of nothing else. She would not be happy until she was rid of her tail and able to join her Prince. So she went to visit the wicked Sea Witch to see if she could help, and they made a terrible deal.

In return for a potion to turn her tail into legs, the little mermaid gave the witch her lovely voice. The witch told her that every step she took would be like walking on knives, and she would never again be a mermaid or be able to return home. But the mermaid could think only of her Prince and agreed to this dreadful demand at once.

The Prince found the little mermaid lying on the steps of his palace the next day. She could not speak, but he welcomed the beautiful stranger to his home, and she soon captivated his court with her sweet smile and graceful dancing.

As the weeks passed the Prince showed nothing but kindness to the mermaid, and grew to love her as dearly as if she were his own sister. He never once thought of marrying her.

And so in time it was arranged that the Prince should marry a neighbouring Princess, and he set off on the Royal Ship to meet her. The Prince was overjoyed, for she was the same girl who had knelt by his side on the beach. "You are the one who saved me!" he cried. The heartbroken little mermaid could only watch in silence, and could not explain the truth.

And so the happy couple were married at once. That night, the sad little mermaid gazed out to sea. Having failed to win his heart, she would soon turn to foam on the sea, as the witch had told her. Just then, her sisters rose up from the waves.

"Take this knife," they called. "The Sea Witch says that if you kill the Prince and let his blood fall on your feet you will become a mermaid again!" But the little mermaid could not kill her Prince for she loved him too much. So she flung the knife far out to sea and jumped overboard. But instead of dissolving into foam, she felt herself being raised into the air by a thousand beautiful spirits and she was filled with joy.

She could see the Prince
and his bride sleeping
peacefully far
below her and she
was truly glad
they had found
happiness
together.

Tom, Tom, The Piper's Son

Tom, Tom, the piper's son,
Stole a pig and away he run!
The pig was eat, and Tom was beat,
And Tom went roaring down the street.

★ Ali Baba and the Forty Thieves ★

In a far away land there lived two brothers. Ali Baba was poor, but his brother Cassim was wealthy and lived in a fine house. He had a greedy wife who always wanted more. One day Ali Baba was working in the forest when he heard some men on horses approaching, and he hid in a tree in case they were robbers. He watched as they stopped by a great rock face.

"Open, Sesame!" cried their leader, and a secret door swung open. Ali Baba counted as they went inside. "Forty robbers! I wonder what they have hidden in that cave." Later the men came out and rode away. Then Ali Baba went and stood by the rock face. "Open, Sesame!" he cried. The rock door slid open and he ran inside.

The cave was full of wonderful treasures – silk and jewels
and great chests of gold coins! Ali Baba was overjoyed!
Now he would never be hungry again. Quickly he took as
much gold as he could carry
and hurried home.
His wife was delighted,
but when his
brother's wife
found out she
was jealous.
Ali Baba told his
brother what had
happened and
offered to share
the treasure.

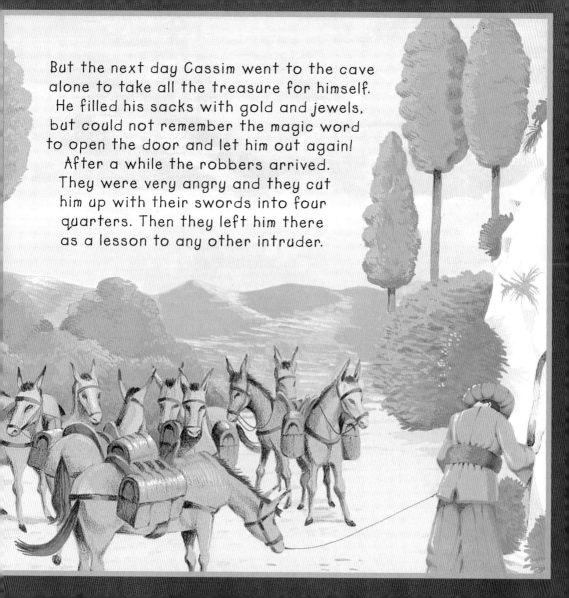

But the next day Cassim went to the cave
alone to take all the treasure for himself.
He filled his sacks with gold and jewels,
but could not remember the magic word
to open the door and let him out again!
After a while the robbers arrived.
They were very angry and they cut
him up with their swords into four
quarters. Then they left him there
as a lesson to any other intruder.

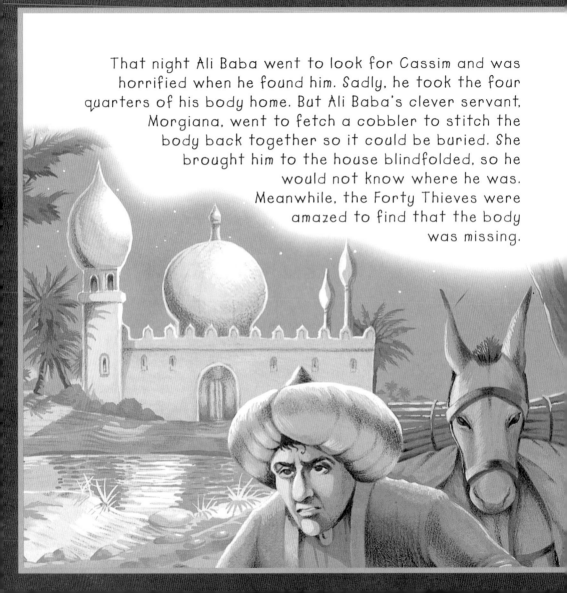

That night Ali Baba went to look for Cassim and was horrified when he found him. Sadly, he took the four quarters of his body home. But Ali Baba's clever servant, Morgiana, went to fetch a cobbler to stitch the body back together so it could be buried. She brought him to the house blindfolded, so he would not know where he was. Meanwhile, the Forty Thieves were amazed to find that the body was missing.

"Someone else knows our secret password!" cried the
Captain. "He must be found!"
One of the robbers was sent to the city. In return for a
gold coin, the cobbler soon led the robber to the very
door, for he remembered the way he had gone, and the
robber marked the door with a cross.
But when Morgiana saw the
cross she guessed what had
happened, and put crosses
on all the other doors so
that when the robbers
returned they could not
find the house.

The next day the Captain himself made the cobbler take him to the house. Then he went to the market, bought forty mules and forty oil jars, and returned to his cave. Each robber climbed inside a jar, and the mules carried the jars to the city.

Disguised as an oil merchant, the Captain went to Ali Baba's house and asked for a bed for the night, and kind Ali Baba agreed. The Captain left his mules in the yard outside, with the men in the jars ready to fight when the Captain gave the word.

But clever Morgiana soon discovered the men and knew they were the robbers come to attack her master. So she boiled a large pan of oil and tipped it over each of the robbers until they were all dead. Later, the Captain went to give the order to fight and found his men killed. He fled over the wall and was gone.

Next day Morgiana told Ali Baba what had happened and he thanked her for saving his life. But the Captain soon made another plan to kill him. This time he disguised himself as a rich cloth merchant and he soon made friends with Ali Baba. But when he arrived for dinner one evening, Morgiana guessed who he was at once. Offering to dance for them, she whirled close to the Captain and taking a dagger from her belt she stabbed him.

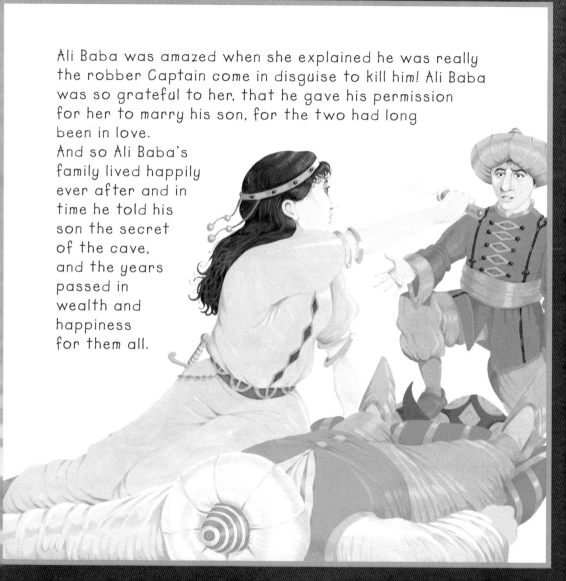

Ali Baba was amazed when she explained he was really the robber Captain come in disguise to kill him! Ali Baba was so grateful to her, that he gave his permission for her to marry his son, for the two had long been in love.
And so Ali Baba's family lived happily ever after and in time he told his son the secret of the cave, and the years passed in wealth and happiness for them all.

THE EMPEROR'S NEW CLOTHES

Many years ago, in a far off land, there lived an Emperor who had a great interest in one thing only – his clothes! He took no interest in his food, his entertainment, his soldiers, or his government. As long as he was beautifully and expensively dressed he was happy, and he would strut about showing off to anyone who cared to watch.

Strangers often visited the large, wealthy city he lived in. One day two men arrived at the city gate. They were dishonest swindlers pretending to be weavers.

"We can weave a cloth more beautiful than you could imagine," they said. "And what is more, it's magical. Only clever people can see it. Stupid people think it's invisible!"

When the Emperor heard their claims, he was curious. "I should like a suit made from this cloth," he thought. "Then I would find out which of my ministers are clever, and which are stupid." So the Emperor gave the men a large bag full of gold coins, and told them to make him some of the magical cloth. The swindlers set up their weaving looms and pretended to start work.

After a while the Emperor was curious to see his new material, but he remembered that only clever people could see it. He decided to find out how clever the Prime Minister was, and sent him along to take a look. But the poor Prime Minister was astonished to find he could see nothing at all! "I must be stupid!" he thought. He would have to pretend he could see the cloth so no-one would find out!

So the Prime Minister told the Emperor it was the most splendid cloth he had ever seen, and the swindlers laughed to think they had fooled him. Next, the Emperor sent the Chancellor to see what he thought.

"Isn't it beautiful?" asked the weavers, holding up a pretend length of cloth.

"L...lovely," stammered the Chancellor, who could see nothing at all. And he went back and told the Emperor that the cloth was superb. The Emperor could wait no longer. He went to see for himself, followed by his courtiers.

"See your Majesty!" cried the Prime Minister and the Chancellor. "Such texture! Such glorious colour!"

The Emperor was amazed for he could see nothing at all. "This is terrible," he thought. "Am I stupid? Am I not fit to be Emperor?" He decided at once to pretend.

"It has my complete approval," he announced. "It is delightful."

His puzzled courtiers gathered round and stared. They, too, saw nothing, but no one wanted to appear stupid. "Exquisite!" they cried.

And so the Emperor ordered a new suit made from the cloth, to wear at the grand procession the next day. He arrived early in the morning, eager to try on the suit.

"It is so soft, your Majesty," said the swindlers, "that it will feel as if you are wearing nothing at all!"

The Emperor took off all his clothes, and the swindlers pretended to dress him. He gazed at the mirror, admiring his fine new suit. "What a perfect fit!" exclaimed his courtiers. "It's a wonderful suit!"

"Splendid!" said the Emperor. And all the time he was really wearing nothing at all!

At last it was time for the procession to begin. The Emperor walked along proudly leading the way, and all the people stared. To their amazement they could see that he was not wearing a stitch of clothing! But no one dared to admit it for fear of being thought stupid. Meanwhile the swindlers packed up, grabbed their bags of gold and fled the city!

Then one little boy piped up, "But the Emperor has nothing on!"

Everyone gasped, but soon they were repeating what he had said. "The Emperor has nothing on!" they whispered, until at last the whole crowd cried out, "The Emperor has lost his clothes!"

The Emperor turned a deep shade of pink all over, for he knew it was the truth. But he was far too proud to admit his foolish vanity, so he just stuck his nose in the air and marched home, with this chamberlains still carrying his invisible train behind him!

Mary, Mary, Quite Contrary

Mary, Mary, quite contrary,
How does your garden grow?
With silver bells and cockle shells
And pretty maids all in a row.

Tom Thumb

Once upon a time there lived a poor woodman and his wife. They were very sad, for they longed to have children of their own.

"How lonely it is!" said the woodman's wife. "I should be happy, even if we had a child who was no bigger than my thumb!"

One day this woman's wish came true, for not long after she had a little boy who was strong and healthy, but no bigger than her thumb.

"I shall call him Tom Thumb," she said.

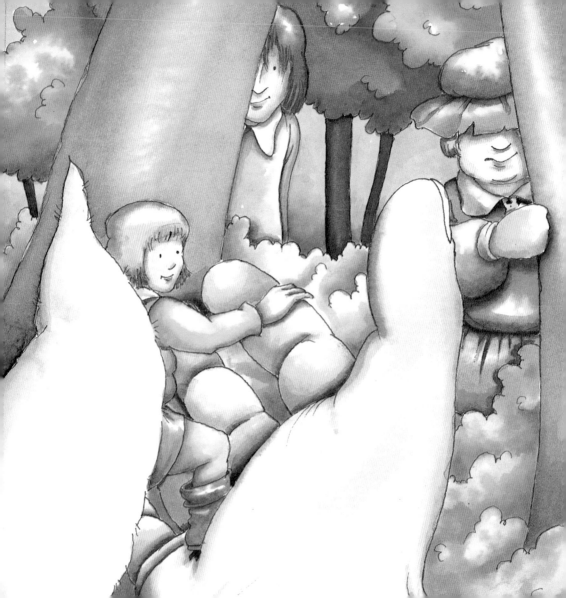

One day Tom was in the forest with his father when two men saw him. They wanted to buy Tom and offered his father a big bag of gold for him, but his father was not happy.

"Take the money," said Tom. "I will soon find a way to come back to you."

So the men took Tom with them, but after a while they let him down to stretch his legs. Quick as a flash, Tom ran into a mouse hole and hid until the men had gone.

That night he slept in an empty snail shell that he found nearby.

Later that night Tom was woken by some robbers who were planning to steal all the gold from the parson's house.

"Hey there!" called Tom. "I can help you!"

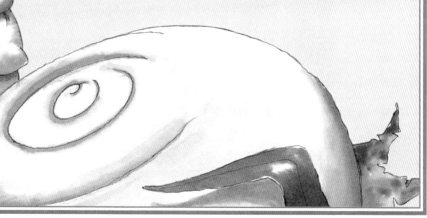

The robbers took Tom to the parson's house, and he crawled through the bars on the window.

"Do you want all the gold ?" Tom yelled. He shouted so loudly that he woke the cook, and the robbers ran off as fast as they could. Tom laughed and laughed. That night he went to sleep in a nice, warm barn.

The next morning Tom woke up and found himself inside a cow's stomach. The cow had not seen him asleep in the hay she was eating.

"Let me out!" he shouted, scaring the poor milkmaid so much that she fell off her stool! Everyone thought the poor cow had gone mad and so it was killed. The cow's stomach was thrown on a rubbish heap where it was eaten by a wolf, so Tom was no better off, but he soon made a plan to escape.

"Hey, Mr Wolf," called Tom. "Are you still hungry?"

The wolf said he was very hungry so Tom directed him to his own house where there was always a lot to eat. That night the wolf crept into the kitchen and helped himself to all the goodies that he found there. But he ate so much that he couldn't fit through the door to get out again!

Tom laughed so loudly that his parents woke up and came running down the stairs.

In no time Tom's father had killed the wicked old wolf with an axe. They cut open his stomach and out jumped their very own Tom Thumb! How pleased they were to see each other again! "Adventures are all very well," said Tom happily. "But there is no place like home!"

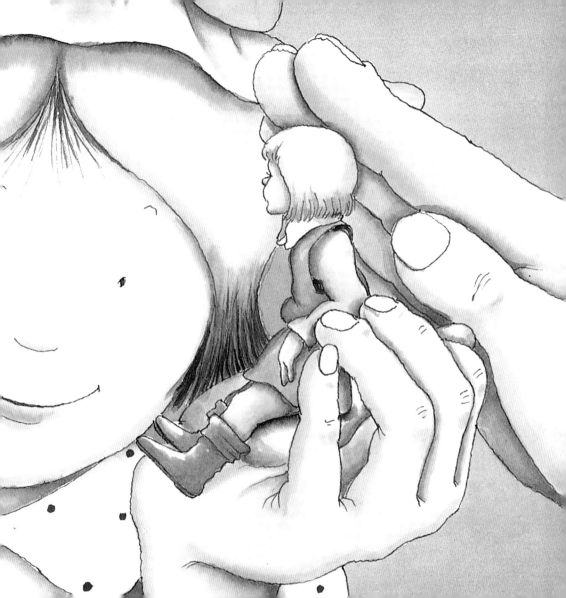

★ The Steadfast Tin Soldier ★

There was once a Tin Soldier. He was exactly the same as his twenty-four brothers, but for one thing. He had only one leg! When he was made, the tin ran out just as it was about to be poured into his second leg, but he could still stand straight and tall.

He lived in the nursery with all the other toys, but his favourite was a pretty little Dancer made of paper. She stood on one toe and pointed her other foot high in the air, almost as if she had only one leg, just like him! The Steadfast Tin Soldier loved to watch her and stood perfectly still for hour after hour gazing at her lovely face and wishing he could find the courage to speak to her.

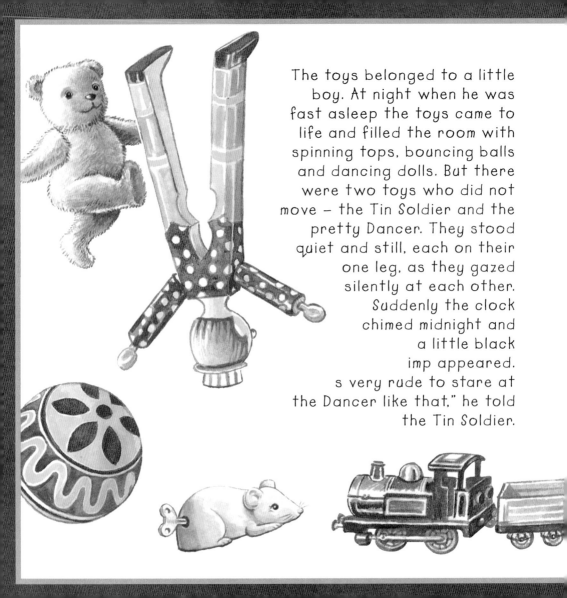

The toys belonged to a little boy. At night when he was fast asleep the toys came to life and filled the room with spinning tops, bouncing balls and dancing dolls. But there were two toys who did not move – the Tin Soldier and the pretty Dancer. They stood quiet and still, each on their one leg, as they gazed silently at each other. Suddenly the clock chimed midnight and a little black imp appeared. s very rude to stare at the Dancer like that," he told the Tin Soldier.

The next day the little boy played with the Tin Soldier and when he went for his tea he left him standing by the window. Now whether it was the wind or whether it was the little black imp up to his tricks, who can say, but all of a sudden the window flew open and the Soldier was blown outside! Down he tumbled and landed with a bump upside down between two paving stones. There he stayed, firmly wedged, and soon it began to rain.

When the rain stopped two little boys
found him, and made a paper boat for
him to sail in, and he whooshed along
the gutter.
All of a sudden the boat entered a
dark tunnel and the boys' excited
shouts were left far behind.

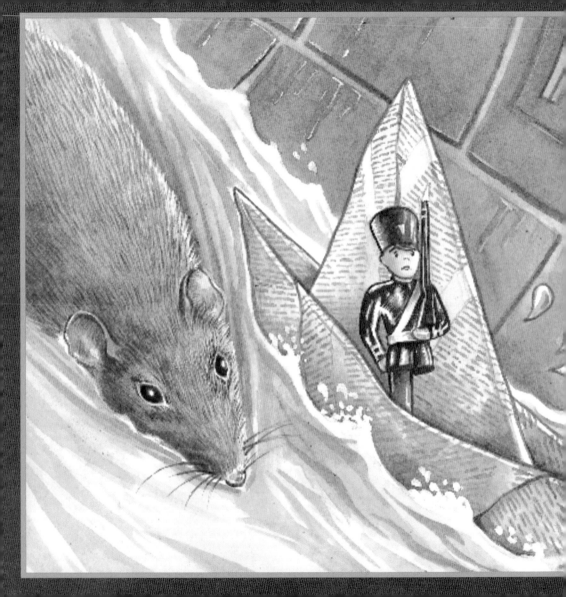

The Tin Soldier felt very frightened, but he stood up straight and tall. Suddenly a great water rat appeared and the Tin Soldier thought his end had come. But the boat sped on out into the light once more and over a great waterfall, for this was where the gutter emptied into the canal. The paper boat fell apart and the Tin Soldier sank below the water, still standing proudly to attention, and thinking only of the little Dancer.

Suddenly the Tin Soldier heard a loud gulp! He had been swallowed by a fish! The fish began to twist this way and that and then all was still once again.

The hours passed and just when the Tin Soldier thought he was lost forever there was a flash of light and he found himself lying on a table. The fish had been caught and taken to market. And now it was lying on a kitchen table, ready to be prepared and cooked.

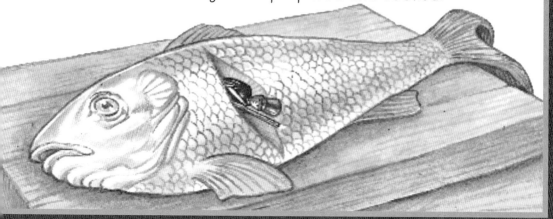

"It's a little Tin Soldier," exclaimed the cook. "I will take him up to the nursery." To his amazement, the Tin Soldier found himself back in his old nursery and there was the pretty Dancer still standing on one toe.

But the little boy was not pleased to see him. Maybe it was because he looked so shabby, or maybe the little black imp had something to do with it, but he snatched up the Tin Soldier and threw him in the fire!

There he stood tall and brave as the flames flickered around him. He looked straight at the Dancer and she looked right back at him. Suddenly the door opened and a draught blew the paper Dancer into the fire where she landed in the arms of the Tin Soldier.

In the grate the next morning the little boy found a whisp of black paper and a small lump of tin in the shape of a heart – all that was left of the Dancer and her Steadfast Tin Soldier

Sing a Song of Sixpence

Sing a song of sixpence,
A pocket full of rye;
Four-and-twenty blackbirds baked in a pie;
When the pie was opened,
The birds began to sing;
Was not that a dainty dish,
To set before a king?

Hansel and Grettel

Once upon a time there was a poor woodcutter who lived in the woods with his two children, and their horrible stepmother. The woodcutter had very little money for food and so all four of them went hungry for much of the time.

Late one night as the two children lay shivering in their beds they heard their stepmother make a terrible suggestion. They could no longer afford to feed their children so they would take them deep into the woods and leave them there so that they would not be able to find their way home. After arguing for many hours their poor father finally agreed to her plan.

Grettel wept bitterly and her brother Hansel comforted her. "I will find a way home, little sister," he said, and he made a plan.

The next morning the children were taken far away into the woods.

"Stay here until we return," said their stepmother. Soon night fell and they were left alone. Poor Grettel sobbed as if her heart would break.

"Dry your eyes," said Hansel. "On the way here I dropped a white pebble on the ground every few steps. See how they shine in the moonlight. We can follow the trail home." Soon they arrived back home.

Their father was overjoyed to see them
for he was ashamed of leaving them,
and their stepmother pretended to
be pleased also.
But that night they overheard
their parents arguing again.
"The children must be got
rid of or we'll all starve,"
said their stepmother.
"We'll take them deeper
into the wood
tomorrow."
Sadly their father
was forced to
give in.

This time Hansel did not have time to collect any white pebbles, so when they were led into the forest he dropped a trail of crumbled bread for them to follow that night. But later when they searched for the crumbs they were alarmed to find them gone, for the birds had eaten every one! Try as they might the frightened children could not find their way home.

Again and again they tried to find a way out of the forest but every path they took led them ever deeper into the wood. Just then Hansel saw a white dove on a branch. The bird sang so sweetly that the children stopped and listened, then followed her as she flew on deep into the heart of the wood, until they came to a little gingerbread cottage. Its roof was made of honey cake and the windows were all of barley sugar!

Soon they were
munching away on parts of
the house and nothing had
ever tasted so delicious.

Suddenly the door flew open and an old woman hobbled out. Hansel and Grettel were terrified but the old lady smiled and invited them inside. She fed them sweet pancakes, then put them to bed under cosy quilts. But when they awoke next day the old lady's kind manner had changed. Her eyes gleamed as she grabbed Hansel's arm. "You will make a tasty morsel for me to eat," she cackled and then the children saw that they had been tricked. The old lady was a witch and she meant to make a meal of them! Laughing cruelly, she bundled Hansel into a cage. "I will fatten you up before I cook you," she hissed and Hansel shook with fear. Every day she told him to hold his finger out, so she could feel how fat he was getting. But her eyesight was terrible and she could not see that he always held out a bone for her to feel. She could not understand how he stayed so thin.

At last the witch could wait no longer.
"Fat or thin, I will eat him as he is," she decided. Poor
Grettel cried and cried, but the witch took no notice.
Pushing Grettel toward the oven, the wicked witch
told her to creep inside and see if it was
hot enough. But Grettel guessed she
was also on the menu and thinking
quickly, asked the witch how
to get inside.
"Silly goose," said the witch,
poking her head into the
oven, "I could easily get in
myself." Grettel gave her a
great shove, and pushed the
witch right inside the oven.
She slammed the door
tight shut, and that was
the end of the wicked
old witch!
Grettel ran straight
to Hansel's cage and
opened the door.
How they rejoiced to
be free once again!

Then the two children explored the cottage, and found chests full of treasure in every corner! They stuffed their pockets to the brim with jewels and Grettel filled her apron.
Soon they were ready and they set off to find their way home. They wandered for hours until at last the wood became more familiar to them. A kind white duck carried them across the river. Then in the distance they saw their father's house, and began to run. Their father was overjoyed to see them. He had not had a single happy hour since he had left them, and in that time their selfish stepmother had died. They emptied out their pockets and precious jewels rolled all over the floor. Their father hugged them and they all laughed for joy.
And so their troubles were ended and they all lived happily ever after.

Rumpelstiltskin

Once there was a poor miller who had a beautiful daughter. One day the King came riding by, and to impress him the miller foolishly boasted that his daughter could spin straw into gold! Now, the King loved gold, and was very greedy, so he ordered the miller to bring the girl to his palace where he would put her to the test.

The King led the girl into a room filled with a huge mound of straw and an old spinning-wheel. "Spin this straw into gold before morning," he said. "Or you will die," and he locked the door behind her.

The poor girl had no idea what to do, so she put her head in her hands and cried.

Suddenly the door opened and in walked a tiny little man. He offered to help in return for a gift, so she gave him her necklace, and in no time at all he spun the straw into gold.

Next morning, the King was delighted. He ordered the poor girl to stay another night and locked her in a larger room with an even bigger pile of straw. The little man appeared again, and this time he spun the straw into gold in exchange for her gold ring. The greedy King was so excited that the next night he locked her in an even larger room with an even bigger pile of straw.

"Spin this into gold before morning and you shall be my Queen!" he said.

For a third time the girl wept until the little man appeared again, but this time she had nothing left to give him. So the little man offered to work in exchange for a promise.

"Promise that if you become Queen you will give me your first-born child," he said. The girl felt she had no other choice, so she agreed and the little man set to work.

"Besides, I may never become Queen, or have children," she thought to herself.

Next morning the King was overjoyed to see so much treasure and he made the girl his wife that very day. The King and Queen lived happily with their great riches and soon the miller's daughter had forgotten all about her promise. Then, one year later, the Queen gave birth to a beautiful baby daughter and she was filled with happiness. But as she sat gently singing to the baby, the door suddenly blew open and in marched the little man.

"I have come to remind you of your promise," he declared. Then the poor Queen remembered the bargain that she had struck long ago in the room full of straw.

"You may have anything else you wish!" she cried.

"Treasure, jewels, gold – just ask and it shall be yours!" But the little man remained firm, and would take nothing else.

Then the Queen sobbed so hard that her tears softened the little man's heart.

"You have three days to discover my name," he said. "Or I will claim your daughter."

So the Queen summoned her messengers, and sent them out to discover the strangest names they could find. When the the little man arrived next day, she asked:

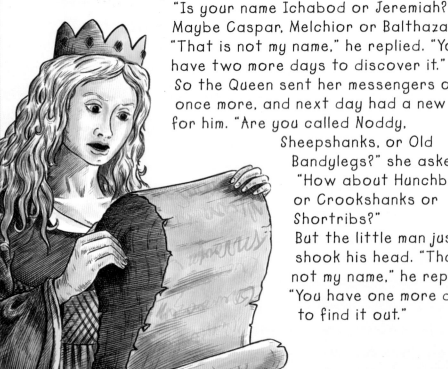

"Is your name Ichabod or Jeremiah? Maybe Caspar, Melchior or Balthazar?"

"That is not my name," he replied. "You have two more days to discover it."

So the Queen sent her messengers out once more, and next day had a new list for him. "Are you called Noddy, Sheepshanks, or Old Bandylegs?" she asked. "How about Hunchback or Crookshanks or Shortribs?"

But the little man just shook his head. "That is not my name," he replied. "You have one more day to find it out."

That evening the Queen sat pale and tired as her messengers read out long lists of names. Then a young messenger burst in, trembling with excitement, and told the Queen he had seen a little man dancing around a fire deep in the woods and singing:

'Merrily the feast I'll make,
Today I'll brew, tomorrow bake.
Merrily I'll dance and sing,
For next day will a stranger bring
The Queen's own child, so fair and sweet,
And then my joy will be complete.
Little does my Lady dream
That Rumpelstiltskin is my name!'

The Queen jumped for joy. At last she had discovered the little man's name!
Next day she teased the little man. "Is your name John? Or Tom? Or Jemmy?"
"It is not," replied the little man.
"Then perhaps it is – Rumpelstiltskin!" cried the Queen.
The little man gnashed his teeth with rage and stomped and screamed. He stamped his feet so hard that the floor gave way beneath him, and he disappeared through it. And that was the end of Rumpelstiltskin!

Diddle, Diddle, Dumpling

Diddle, diddle, dumpling, my son John,
Went to bed with his trousers on;
One shoe off, one shoe on,
Diddle, diddle, dumpling, my son John.

The Sorcerer's Apprentice

Once there was a man who had so much work that he was busy from sunrise to sunset. So he went to town to find an apprentice to help in his workshop.

"Can you read and write?" the man asked a young boy, who was looking for work.

"Why, yes!" replied the boy, who was called Hans.

"What a pity!" sighed the man. "I don't want an apprentice who can read and write." Hans thought quickly. "I can't read or write. I thought you said eat and fight!"

"Excellent!" cried the man. "Then you are just the boy for me."

They set off into the forest, and walked until they reached a dark castle. Now, Hans had only pretended not to read and write, and was curious to find out why the man wanted an ignorant helper.

But when the man led him into his workshop, it soon became clear! Inside there was a huge black cauldron hanging over a fire. Bookshelves were filled with dusty books, jars of strange objects covered the floor, and in the corner was a tall pointed hat! The man was a sorcerer, and Hans guessed he did not want an apprentice who could read his spells! So he pretended to be stupid, while trying to learn all he could. Hans did many jobs for his master. He stirred the foul mixtures bubbling in the cauldron. He ground up herbs — and other nasty things! He swept the workshop, tended the fire and gathered strange ingredients for the magician's potions. But the job he hated most of all was filling the huge cauldron with water. It was so wide and deep that it needed bucket after bucket and each one had to be fetched from a well deep in the deepest dungeon of the castle.

Hans longed to look at the magic books, but he didn't dare as he had told the magician that he could not read or write. Then one day the sorcerer went out, saying he would return that night. "Take good care of my workshop!" he ordered.

As soon as he was gone, Hans took down a big spellbook and had soon found an interesting spell – "How to find an Extra Pair of Hands." Hans looked at the empty cauldron that was waiting to be filled with

water. If only he had an extra pair of hands he could do the job in no time. Following the spell, he fetched a broom, and said the magic words. Suddenly it grew two arms from its handle and stood up straight on its bristles. With a cry of delight Hans handed it two buckets. "Fetch me water from the well and fill the empty cauldron!" he commanded and instantly the broom marched out of the room and down the steps to the dungeon.

Soon Hans could hear it climbing back up the steps and it appeared with two full buckets which it tipped into the huge cauldron. He clapped his hands with glee. The broom made trip after trip and soon the cauldron was full to the brim.

"That's enough!" said Hans, but the broom kept on going. "No more! Stop!" cried Hans, but the broom had been told to fetch water and that is what it was doing! Soon the cauldron was overflowing and had spilled all over the floor.

Hans searched frantically through the spellbook for the magic word to stop the spell, but he could not find a clue. So he grabbed an axe and chopped the broom in two. But to his alarm, each half grew arms and buckets and set off back down the steps. He raced after them and smashed the wood into tiny splinters. But each splinter grew, and formed arms and buckets and soon a whole army was marching down the steps.

Hans ran around in a panic. He tried to block the door but the marching brooms were too strong and pushed him aside. Soon the whole workshop was awash. The poor sorcerer's apprentice put his head in his hands and wept as the water swirled around him. Then suddenly he heard the castle door creak open. The sorcerer had returned! His eyes shone angrily as he entered his watery workshop, and poor Hans shook in his boots. The sorcerer waved his wand, uttered some magic words, and in a flash the brooms disappeared. The water swirled out of the workshop and back into the well. Ashamed, Hans bowed his head as he explained what had happened. But to his great surprise, the sorcerer laughed. "I was young once," he said, "and I was just as curious as you. I will teach you to become a great sorcerer like me on one condition — no more spells until you are ready!" and this time Hans quite happily agreed!

JACK AND THE BEANSTALK

Once upon a time there lived a poor widow and her lazy son Jack. He would not work, and so there came a time when they had no money left for food.

"All we have left to sell is our cow," said Jack's mother, and so the next day Jack took the cow to market, where he sold her for a handful of beans. He took the beans home to his mother, but she was so angry that she threw them out of the window.

"We cannot live on a handful of beans!" she cried, and they went to bed that night very hungry indeed. But when Jack woke next morning all he could see from his window were huge green leaves. The beans had grown into a giant beanstalk, which reached high into the sky.

"I am going to climb up and see where it ends," decided Jack, and began to climb.

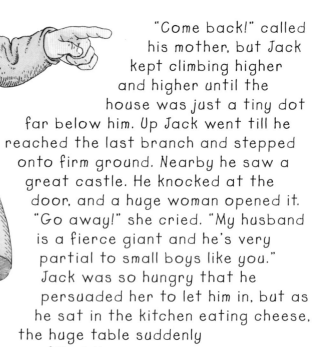

"Come back!" called his mother, but Jack kept climbing higher and higher until the house was just a tiny dot far below him. Up Jack went till he reached the last branch and stepped onto firm ground. Nearby he saw a great castle. He knocked at the door, and a huge woman opened it. "Go away!" she cried. "My husband is a fierce giant and he's very partial to small boys like you." Jack was so hungry that he persuaded her to let him in, but as he sat in the kitchen eating cheese, the huge table suddenly shook and a loud roar filled the air. "Fee, fi, fo, fum, I smell the blood of an Englishman! Be he alive or be dead, I'll grind his bones to make my bread!" "Hurry up and hide!" whispered the terrified woman. "My husband is coming!" She bundled Jack into the oven as an enormous giant strode into the kitchen.

"It's just the smell of your breakfast, dear!" said his wife anxiously. Jack sat silently trembling as the giant gobbled his breakfast, then told his wife to fetch his hen.

"Lay!" ordered the giant and to Jack's astonishment the hen laid an egg at once. But this was no ordinary egg – it was a golden egg! The giant smiled greedily. Then he yawned loudly, laid his great head upon his arms, and was soon fast asleep. Jack leapt out of the oven and grabbed the hen, then he raced from the kitchen and out of the huge castle door.

He ran for the beanstalk as fast as his legs could carry him and in no time at all he was back home with the hen still tucked tightly beneath his arm. "Look, mother!" he cried. "This hen will lay as many golden eggs as we wish. We need never go hungry again."

After a time Jack grew eager for adventure, so disguising himself, he climbed the beanstalk, and persuaded the giant's foolish wife to let him in once more. But as he sat at the kitchen table, he heard a roar:

"Fee, fi, fo fum, I smell the blood of an Englishman!" The giant was coming! Quickly Jack ran and hid in the oven. He peeked out as the giant gulped down his meal.

"Bring me my money bags!" cried the giant.

Slowly he counted piles of glittering golden coins but then he began to yawn and soon he was fast asleep. Jack jumped out of his hiding place, heaved a large money bag over his shoulder and ran like the wind away from the castle.

His mother was very thankful to see him safe and sound and what fun they had that night as they counted their new riches over and over again.

But after a time Jack grew restless, so disguising himself again, he climbed the beanstalk once more. The giant's wife was wary, as she had been tricked twice already, but Jack soon charmed her and she let him in again. This time he tried to steal the giant's golden harp, which played the sweetest music Jack had ever heard. But as he ran from the room, the harp called out,

"Master! Master!" With a cry of rage the giant awoke and stumbled after Jack. Out of the castle and down the beanstalk the terrified boy ran, with the giant close behind him.

"Quick, mother, fetch the axe!" Jack shouted as he neared the ground. He swung the axe high in the air and with one mighty blow felled the plant. The giant gave a loud cry, then tumbled from its branches and landed headfirst on the ground, stone dead. And from that time on Jack and his mother lived happily ever after.

Little Jack Horner

Little Jack Horner,
Sat in a corner,
Eating a Christmas pie.
He put in his thumb,
And pulled out a plum,
And said, "What a good boy am I."